RECORDED VERSIONS
GUITAR ®

AUTHENTIC TRANSCRIPTIONS
WITH NOTES AND TABLATURE

MEGADETH

RISK

4 INSOMNIA

10 PRINCE OF DARKNESS

19 ENTER THE ARENA

20 CRUSH 'EM

28 BREADLINE

34 THE DOCTOR IS CALLING

43 I'LL BE THERE

52 WANDERLUST

62 ECSTASY

70 SEVEN

83 TIME: THE BEGINNING

89 TIME: THE END

95 *GUITAR NOTATION LEGEND*

MUSIC TRANSCRIPTIONS BY COLIN HIGGINS,
MATT SCHARFGLASS, AND PETE BILLMANN

PHOTOGRAPHY BY MYRIAM SANTOS-KAYDA
COURTESY OF CAPITOL RECORDS

ISBN 0-634-01259-2

HAL•LEONARD®
CORPORATION

7777 W. BLUEMOUND RD. P.O. BOX 13819 MILWAUKEE, WI 53213

Visit Hal Leonard Online at
www.halleonard.com

Insomnia

Words and Music by Dave Mustaine

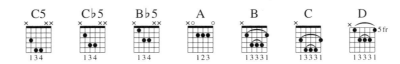

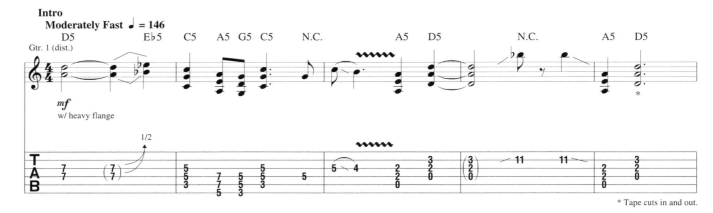

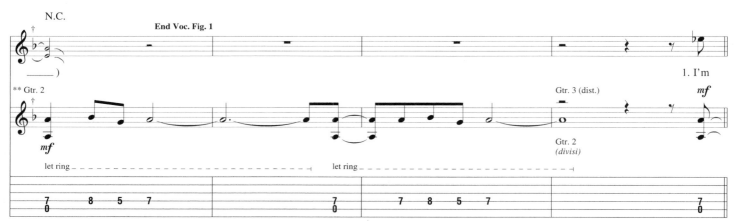

** Sitar arr. for gtr.
† Key signature denotes A Phrygian.

Gtrs. 3 & 4: w/ Rhy. Figs. 1 & 1A, simile

- y past I've ___ bur - ied.   My mind ___ won't let me ___ sleep.   2. I'll   do

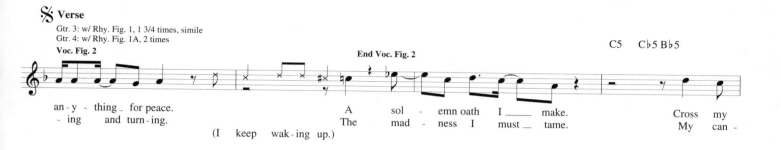

Verse

Gtr. 3: w/ Rhy. Fig. 1, 1 3/4 times, simile
Gtr. 4: w/ Rhy. Fig. 1A, 2 times

Voc. Fig. 2   End Voc. Fig. 2

an - y - thing ___ for peace.   A   sol - emn oath   I ___ make.   Cross   my
- ing   and turn - ing.   The   mad - ness   I   must ___ tame.   My   can -
(I   keep   wak - ing   up.)

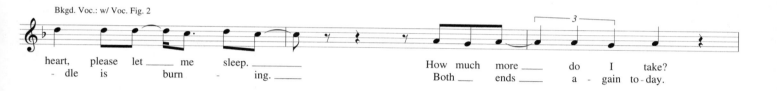

Bkgd. Voc.: w/ Voc. Fig. 2

heart,   please   let ___ me   sleep. ___   How   much   more ___ do   I   take?
- dle   is   burn   ___   ing. ___   Both ___ ends ___ a - gain to - day.

C5   Cb5 Bb5   Pre-Chorus
                           * A5   N.C.   G6   N.C.
                           **

Spoken: I   hear   a   voice   talk - ing   to   me   I   don't ___ know what it   needs.
       Spoken: The   whole   house   is   creak - ing.   I   know they're

Gtr. 3   † Gtr. 1
                           *
                           mf
                           w/ flanger

* Chord symbols reflect implied tonality.
** Key signature denotes A Dorian.
† Synth. arr. for gtr.

A5   N.C.   G6   N.C.   Bm   N.C.   Asus2   N.C.

But the   loud - est   voice ___ is   the   one ___ I   heed. ___
out   there.   The things   kept from sight.   I beg to the shad - ows.

5

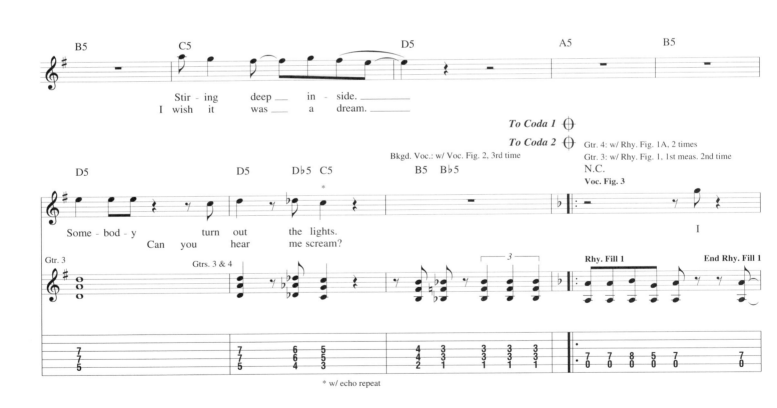

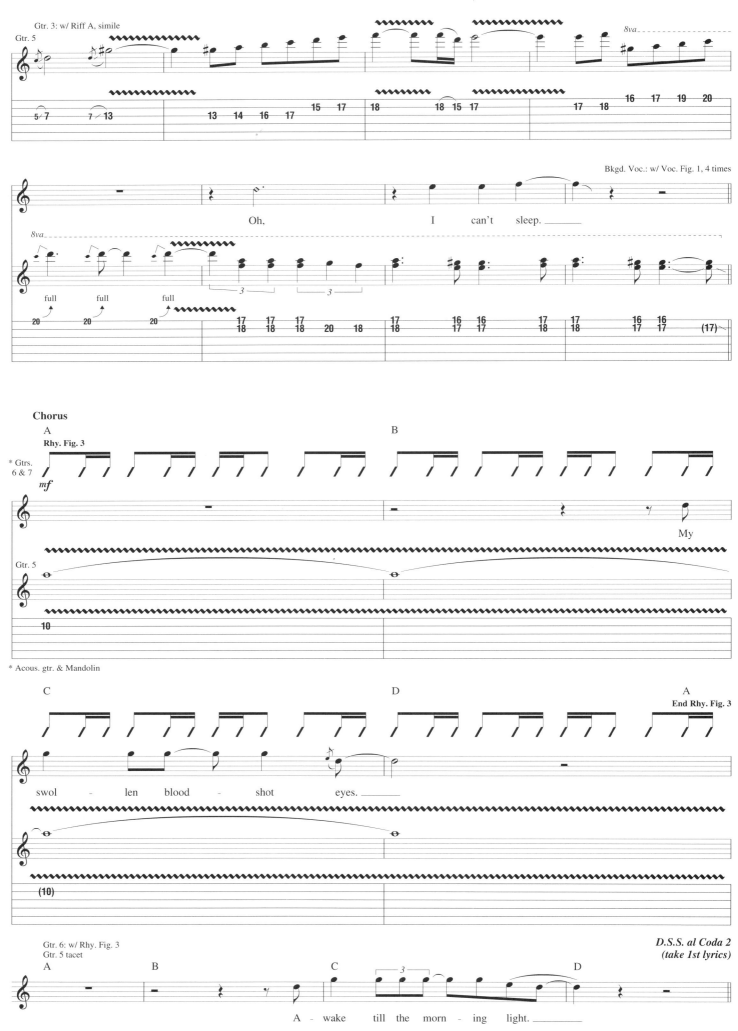

Coda 2
Outro

Prince of Darkness

Words and Music by Dave Mustaine, Marty Friedman and Bud Prager

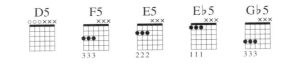

Drop D Tuning:
① = E ④ = D
② = B ⑤ = A
③ = G ⑥ = D

Intro
Moderately ♩ = 124

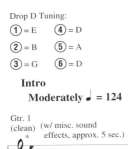

* Key signature denotes D Dorian.

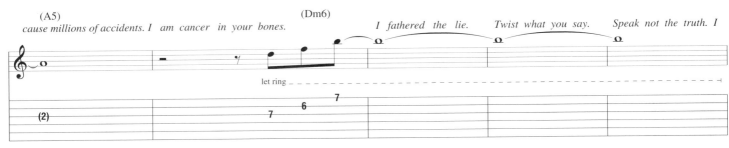

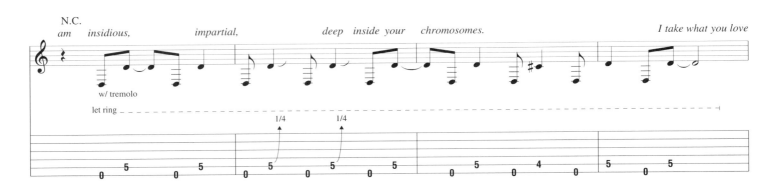

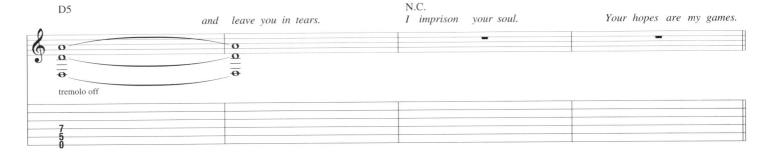

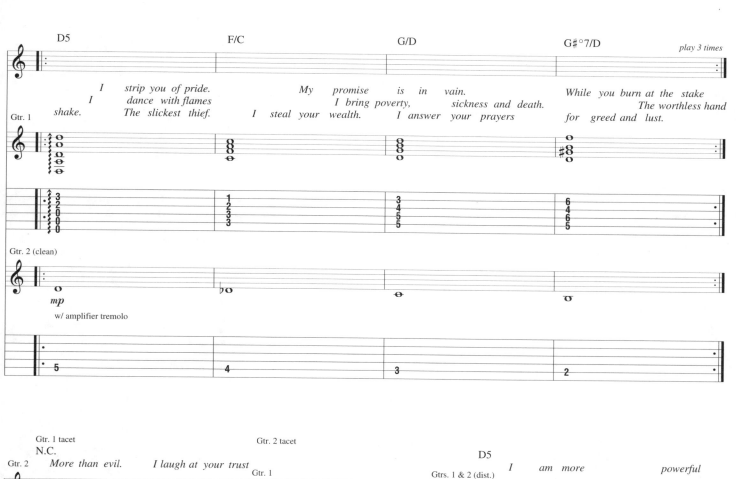

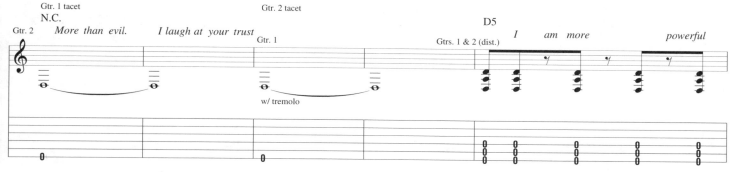

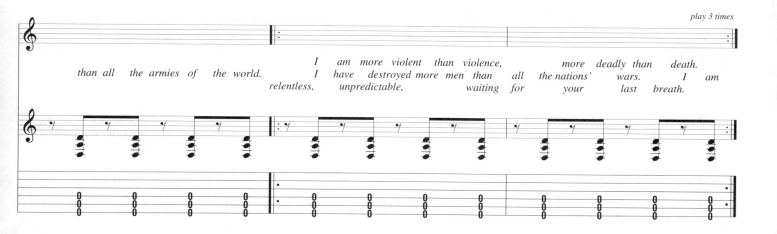

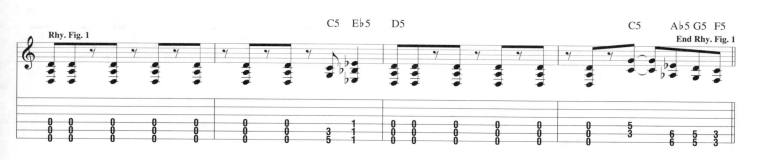

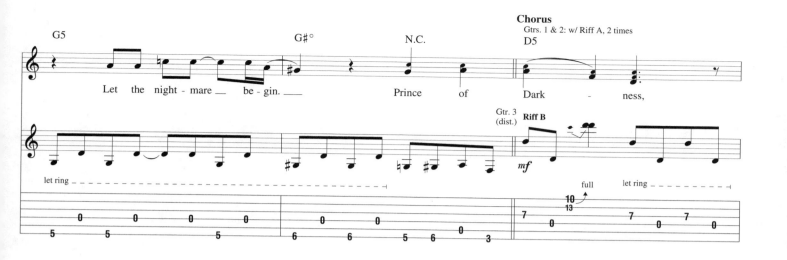

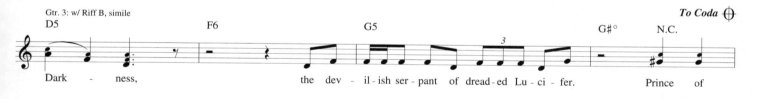

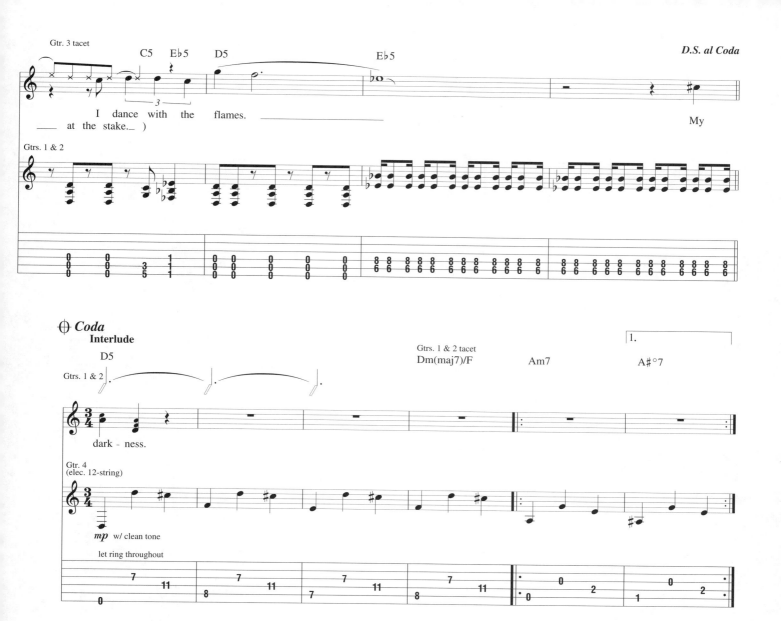

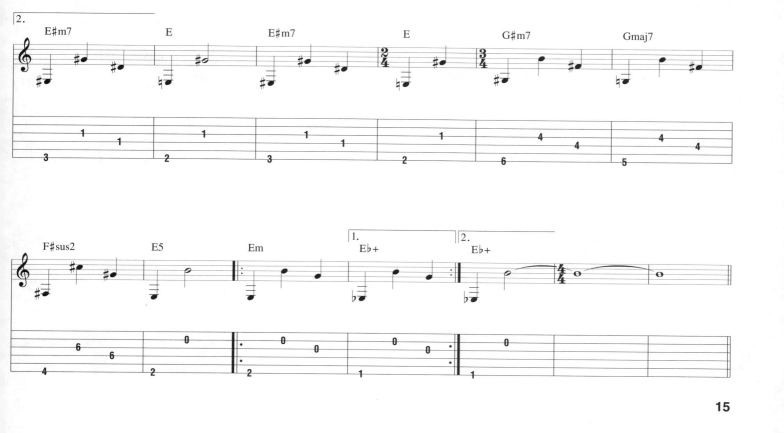

* Hypothetical fret location

* Hypothetical fret location

Enter the Arena

Words and Music by Dave Mustaine, Marty Friedman and Bud Prager

Crush 'Em

Words and Music by Dave Mustaine, Marty Friedman and Bud Prager

Chorus

Breadline

Words and Music by Dave Mustaine, Marty Friedman and Bud Prager

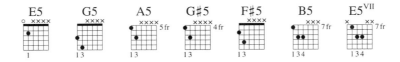

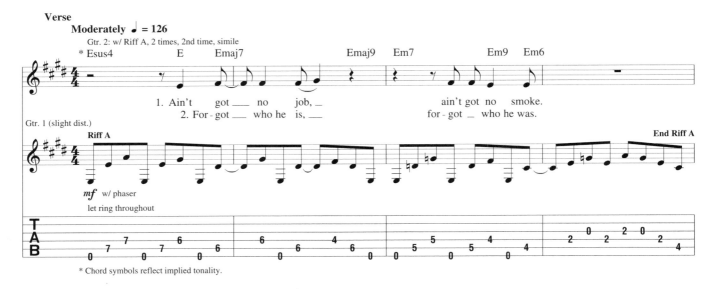

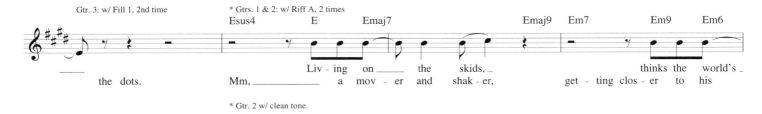

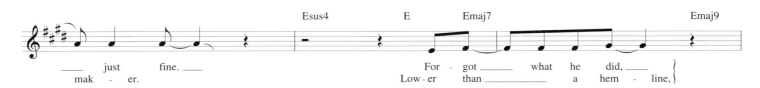

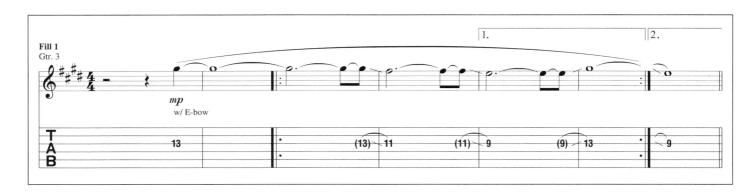

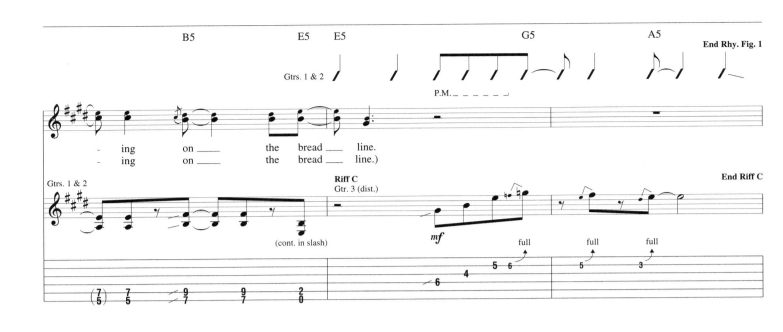

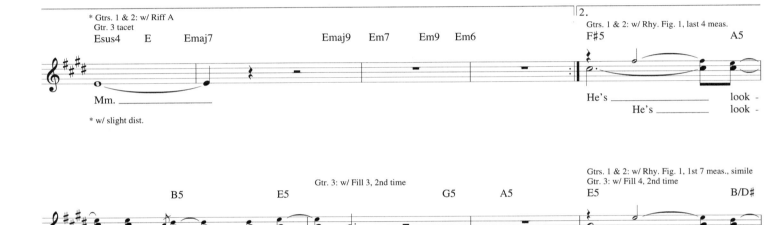

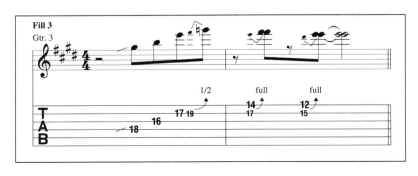

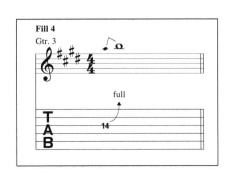

The Doctor Is Calling

Words and Music by Dave Mustaine, Marty Friedman and Bud Prager

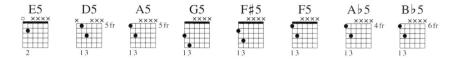

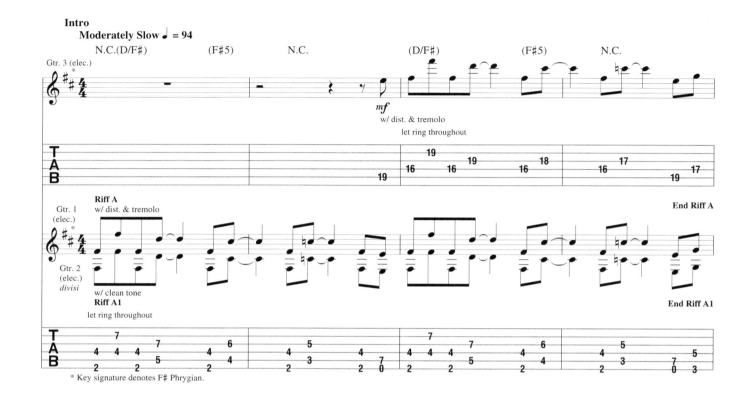

* Key signature denotes F♯ Phrygian.

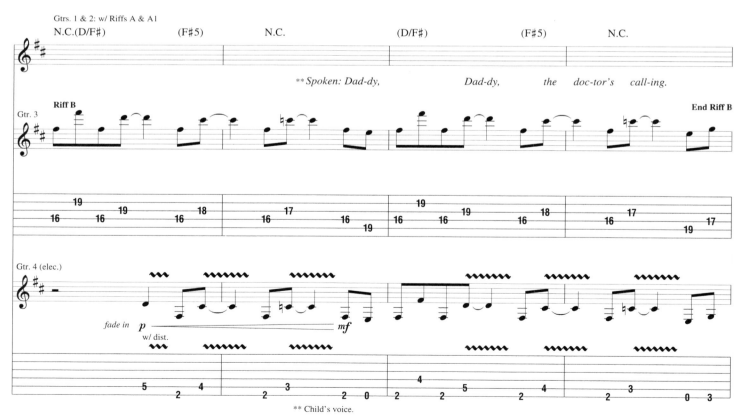

** Child's voice.

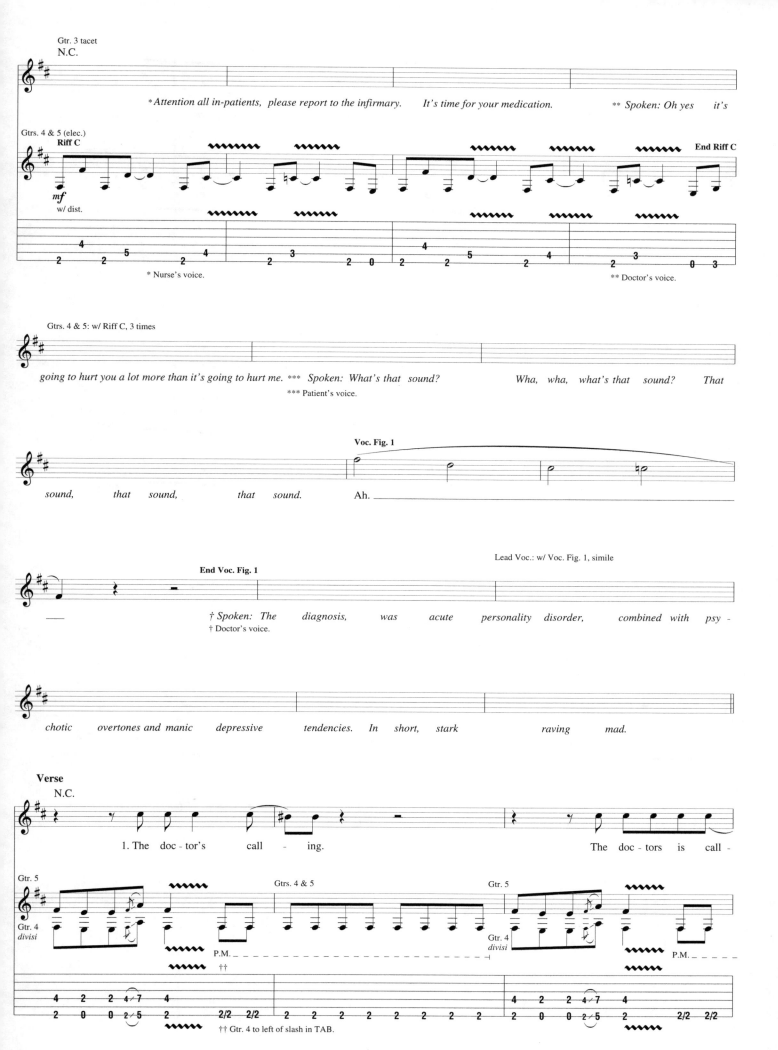

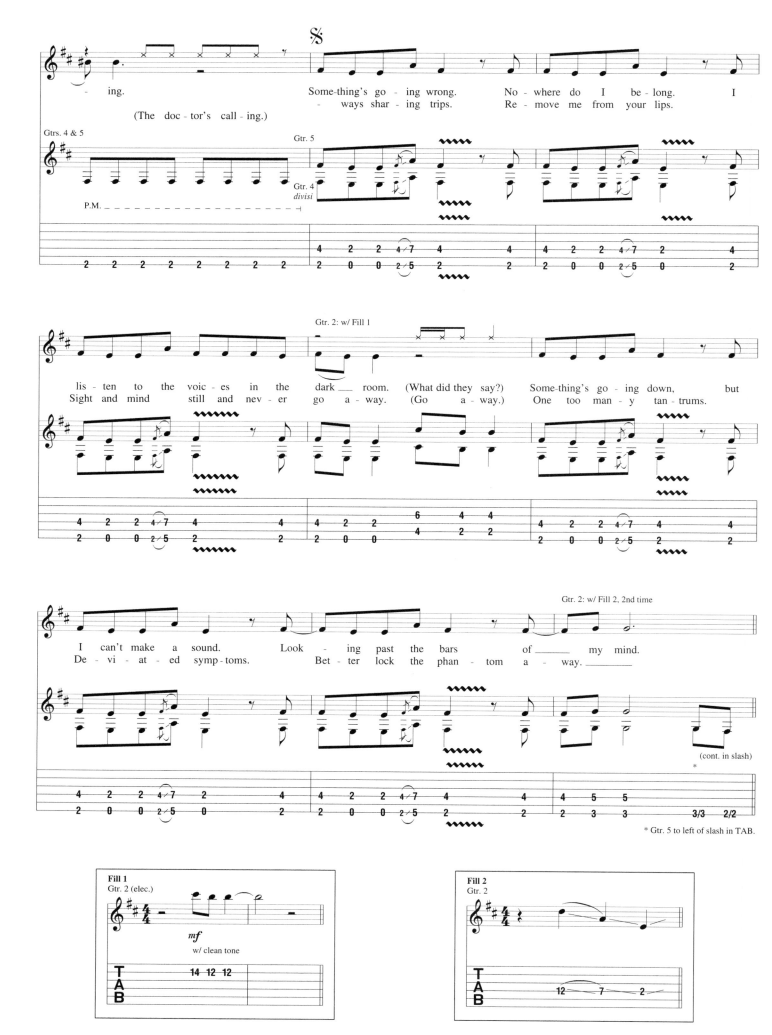

free.   *The doctor's prescription, less   for you and more for me.*

* Microphonic fdbk., not caused by string vibration.
   pitch: A#, C#

Guitar Solo

Na, na, na, na,   na, na, na,   na, na, na,   na, na, na,   na, na, na,   na, na, na,

na, na, na,   na, na, na,   na, na, na,   na, na, na,   na, na, na,   na, na, na,

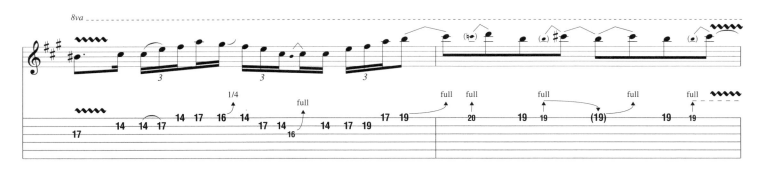

I'll Be There

Words and Music by Dave Mustaine, Marty Friedman and Bud Prager

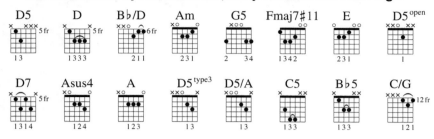

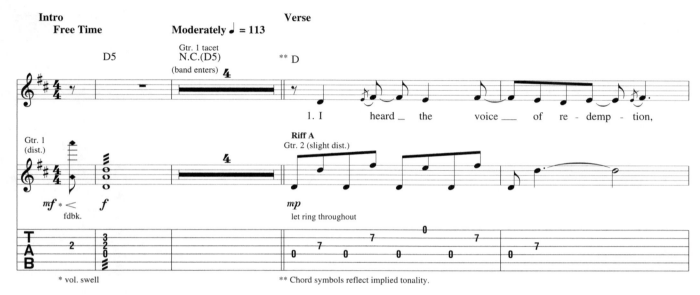

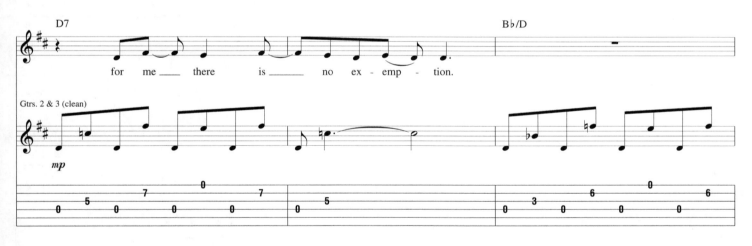

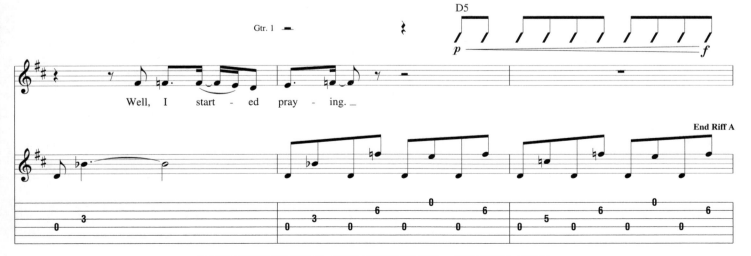

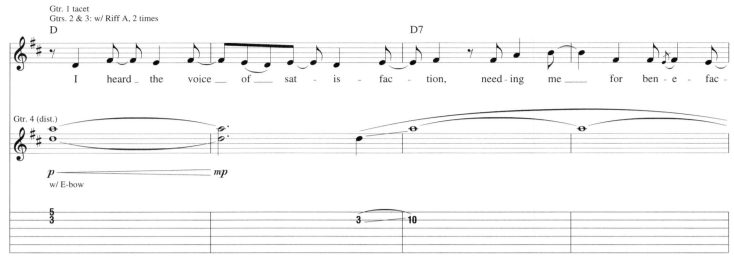

Chorus

Am   G5   Fmaj7#11   G5

I'll be there for you when you walk _ through the fire. _

Am   G5   Fmaj7#11   G5

I'll be there for you _ when the flames _ get high-er. When noth-

Wanderlust

Words and Music by Dave Mustaine, Marty Friedman and Bud Prager

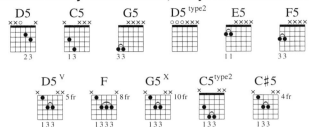

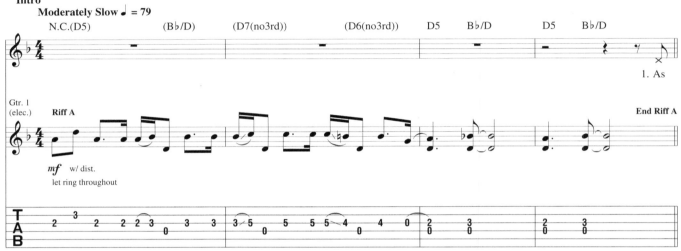

Gtr. 5; Drop D Tuning:
① = E ④ = D
② = B ⑤ = A
③ = G ⑥ = D

Intro
Moderately Slow ♩ = 79

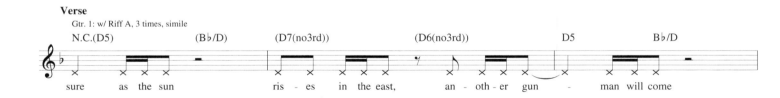

Verse

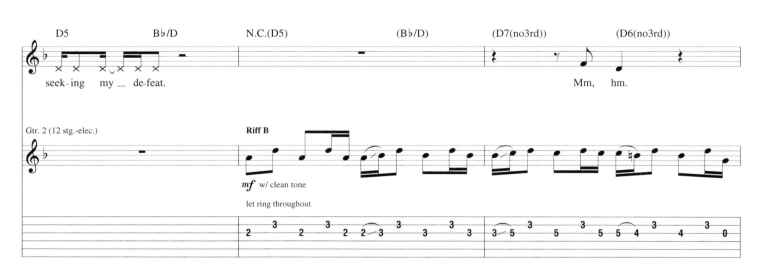

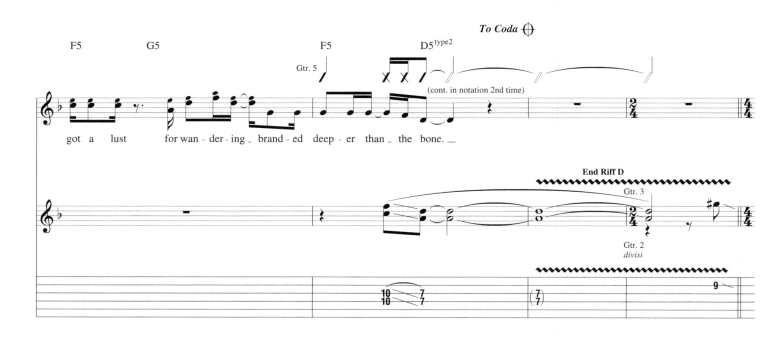

Verse

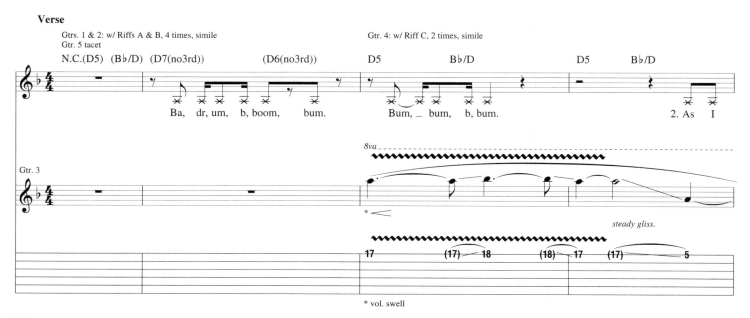

* vol. swell

54

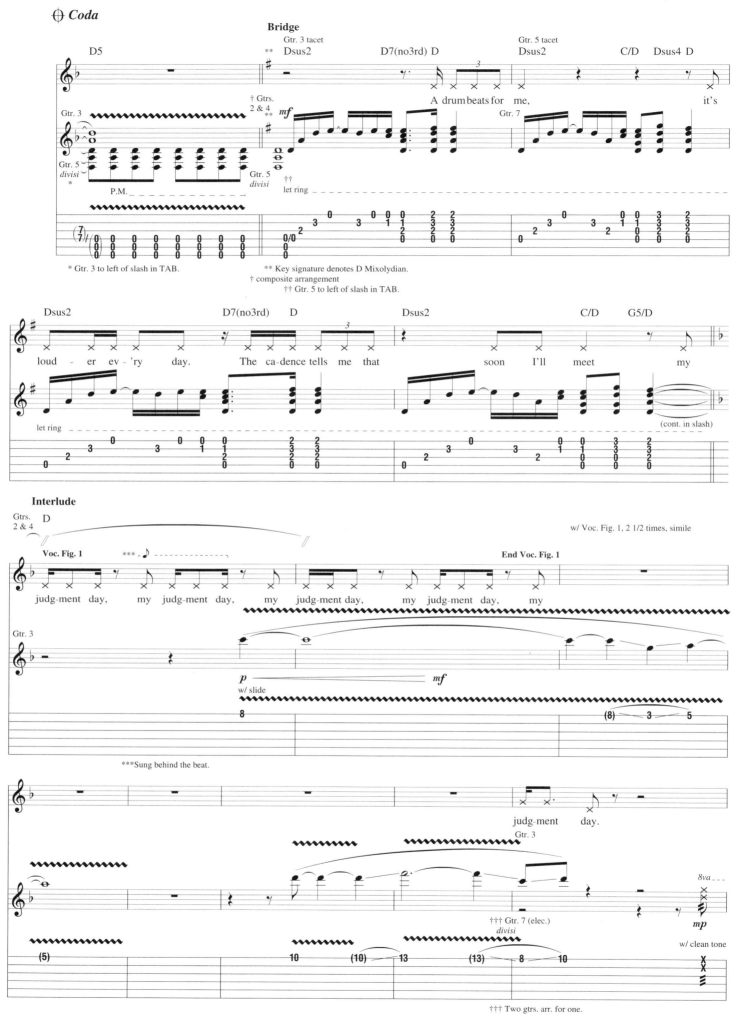

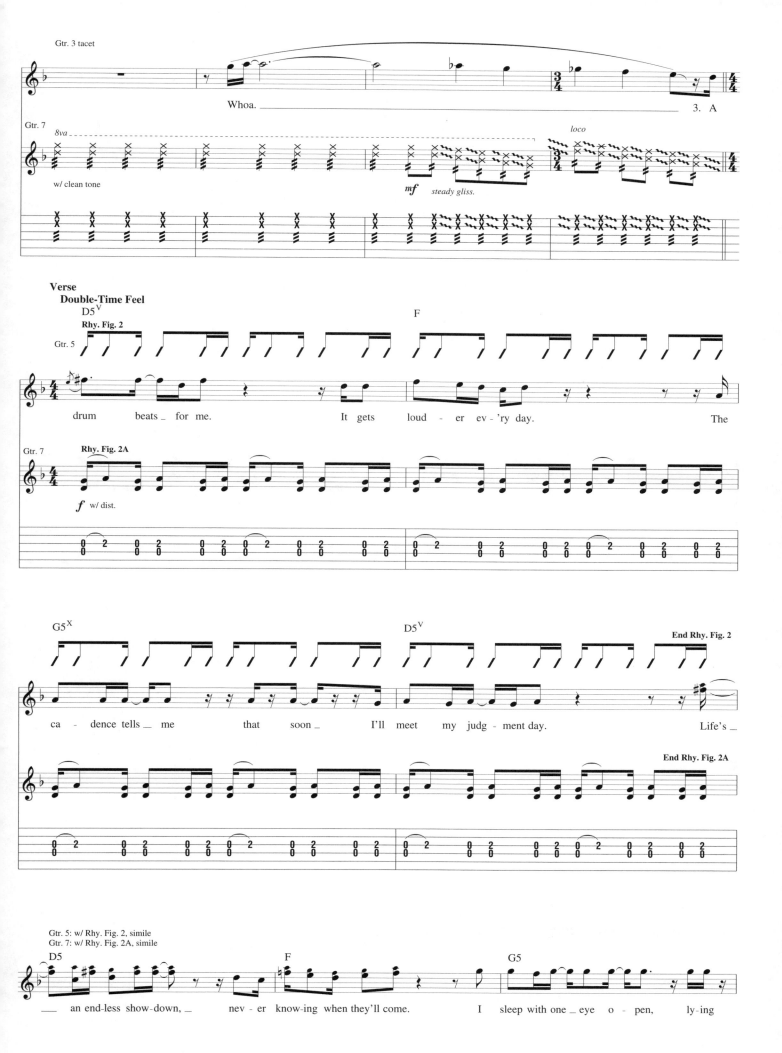

Guitar Solo

Gtr. 5: w/ Rhy. Fig. 2, simile

Gtrs. 2 & 4: w/ Rhy. Fig. 2A, simile

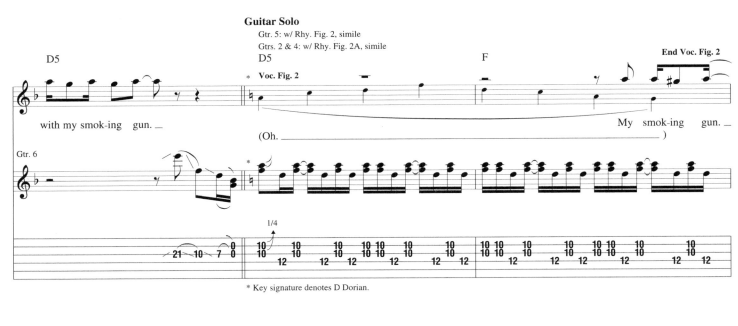

* Key signature denotes D Dorian.

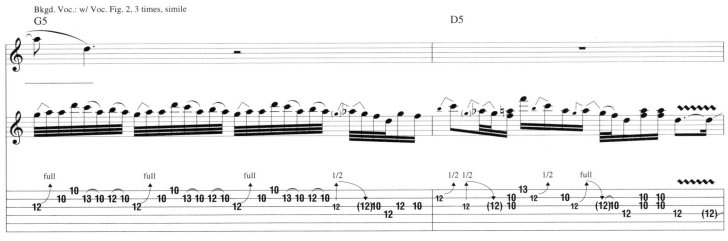

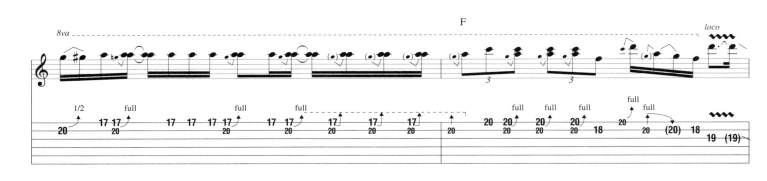

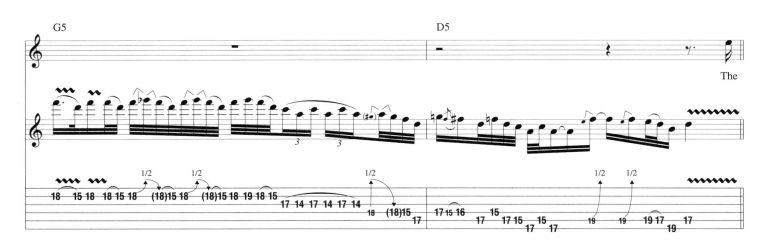

58

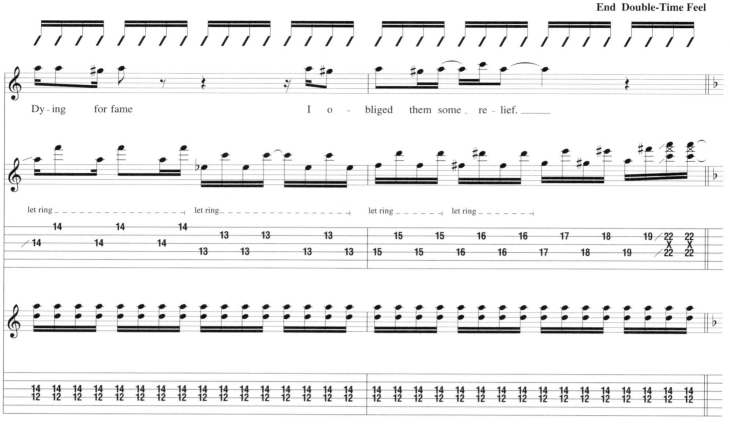

Chorus
Gtr. 3: w/ Riff D, 1st 8 meas., simile
Gtr. 5: w/ Rhy. Fig. 1, 2 times, simile
Gtr. 7 tacet

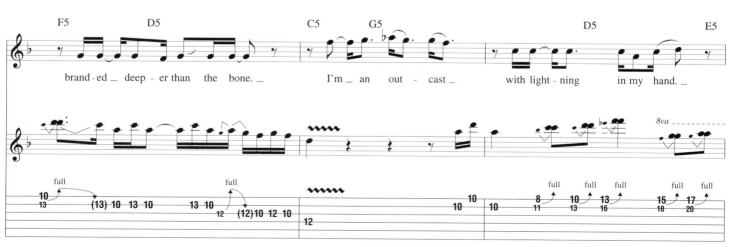

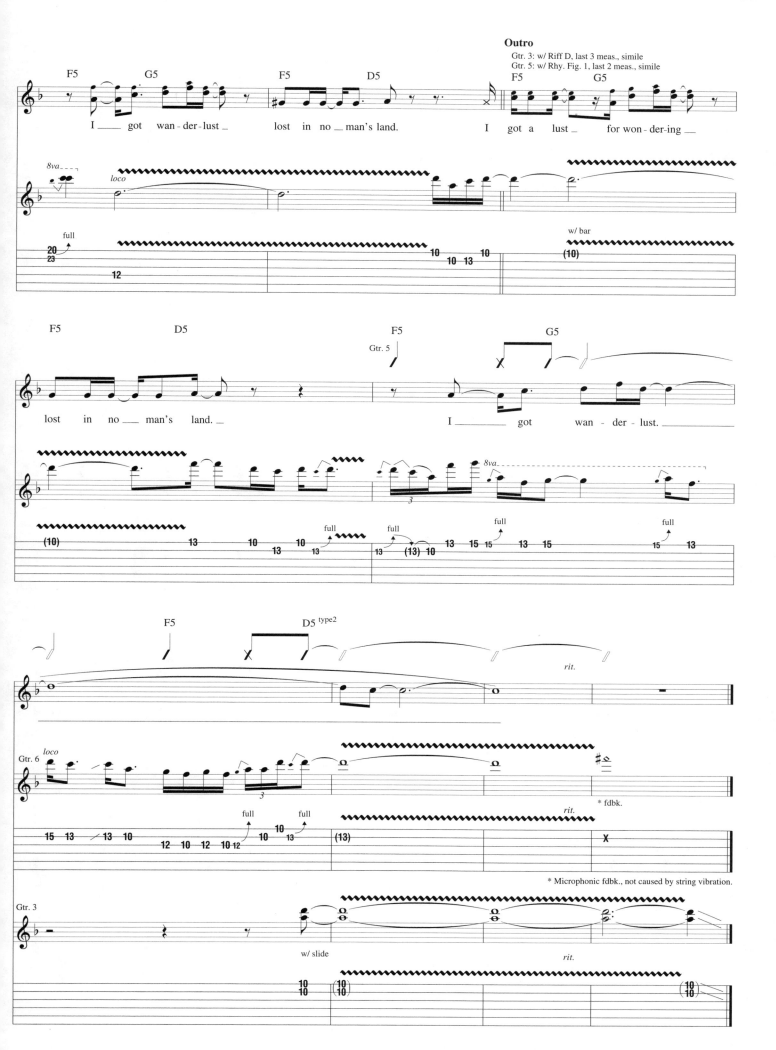

Ecstasy

Words and Music by Dave Mustaine, Marty Friedman and Bud Prager

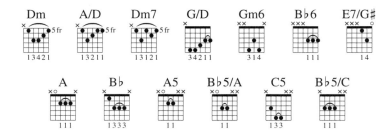

Intro
Moderately Fast Rock ♩ = 129

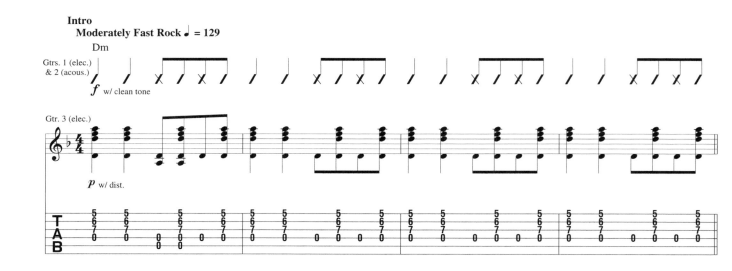

Verse

1.You live ___ in a world ___ of fan - ta - sy, ___ mm. ___

Seven

Words and Music by Dave Mustaine and David Ellefson

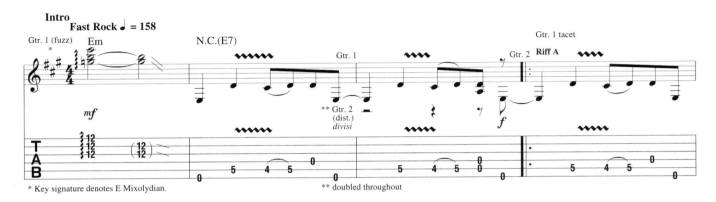

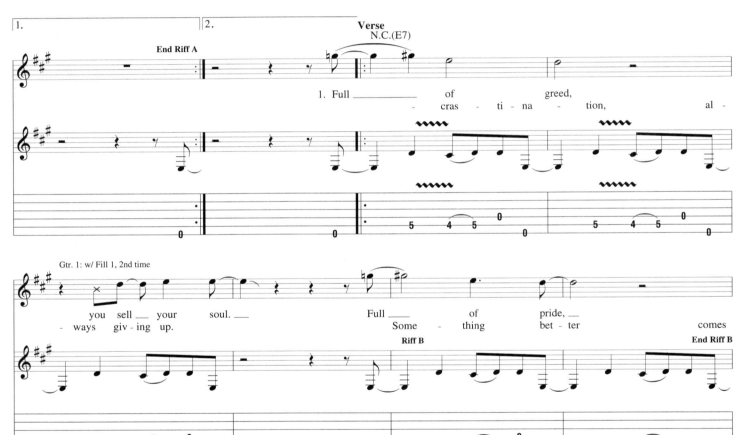

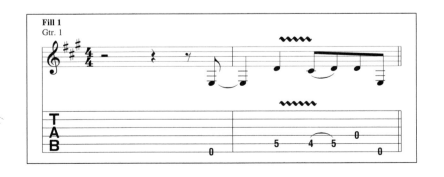

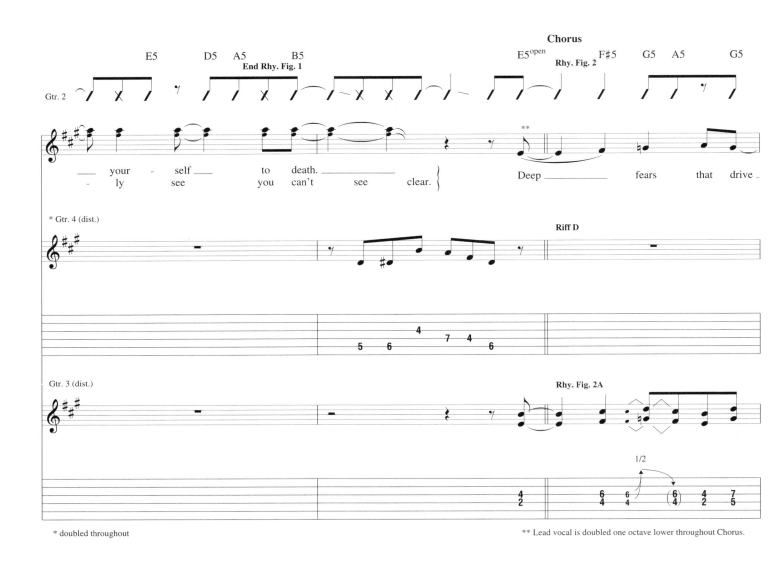

* doubled throughout

** Lead vocal is doubled one octave lower throughout Chorus.

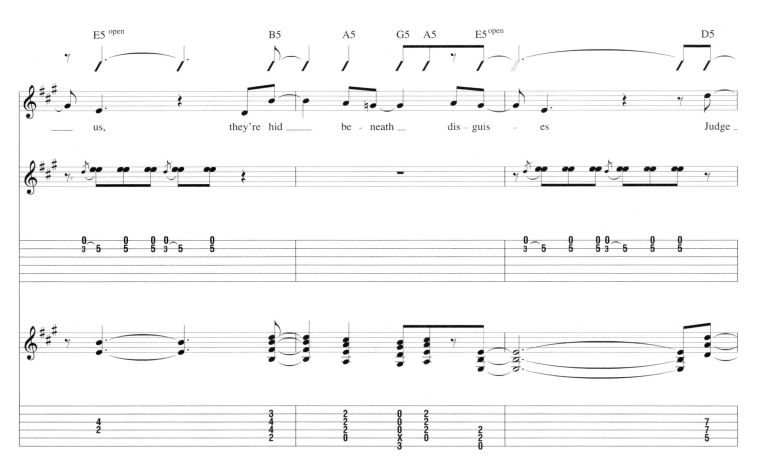

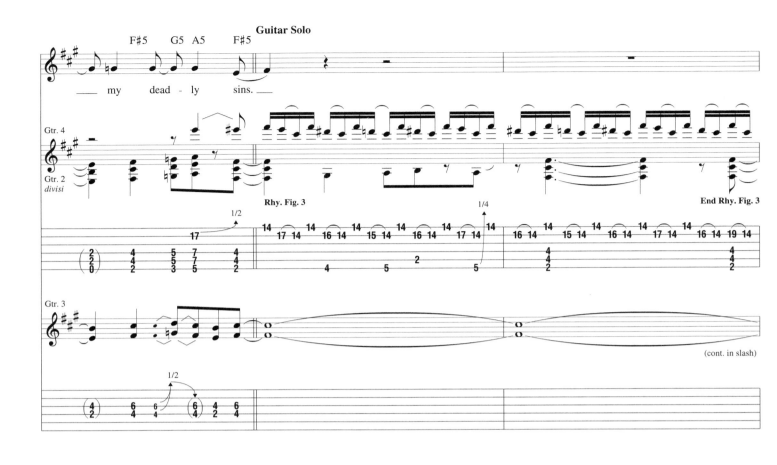

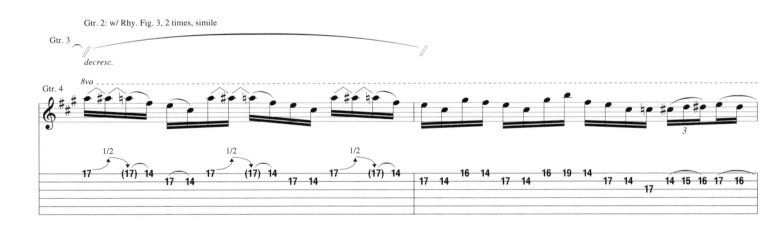

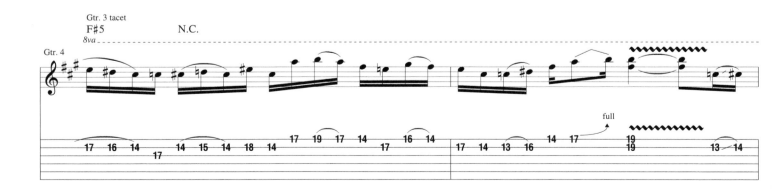

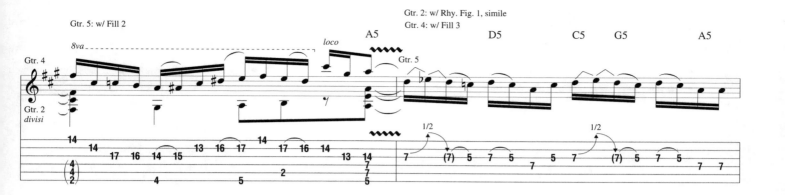

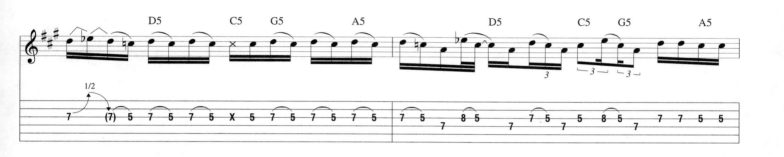

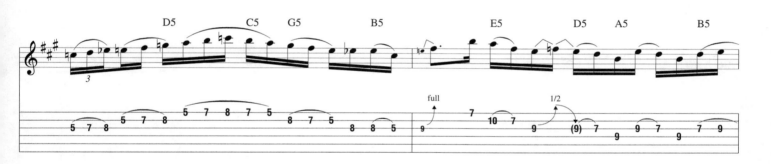

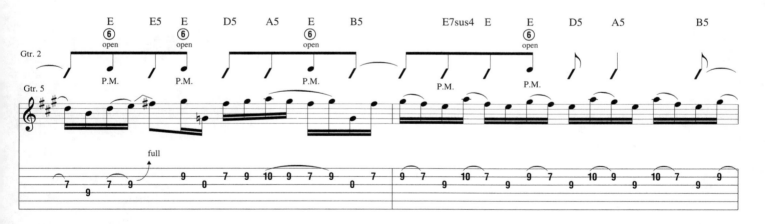

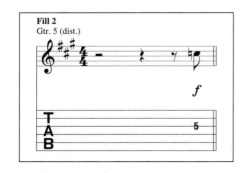

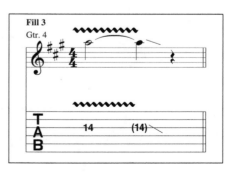

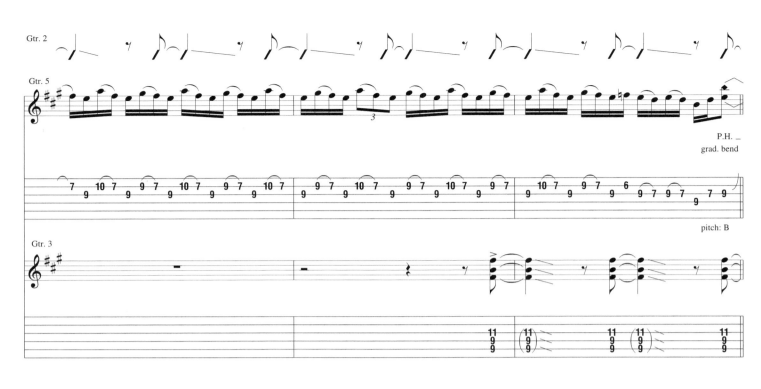

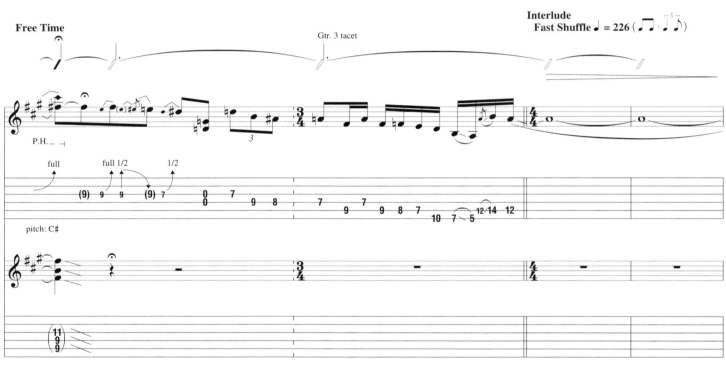

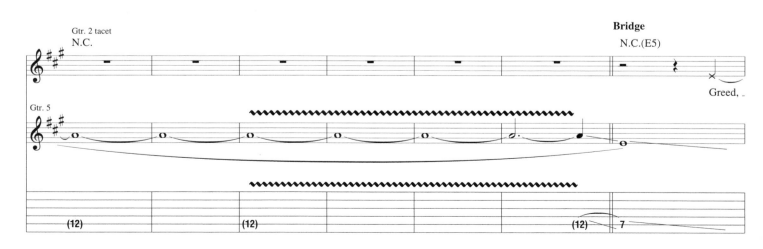

Greed,

glut - to - ny, ___ pride,

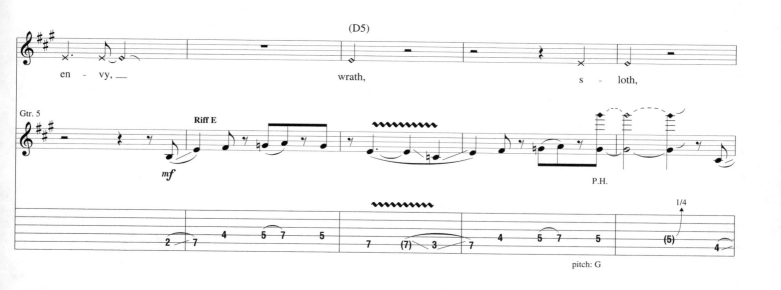

en - vy, ___ wrath, s - loth,

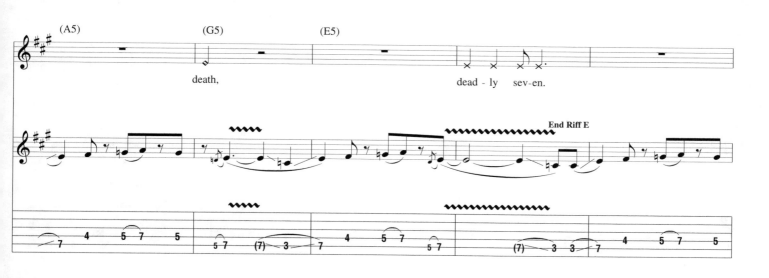

death, dead - ly sev-en.

Sev - en dead - ly sins of mine. ___

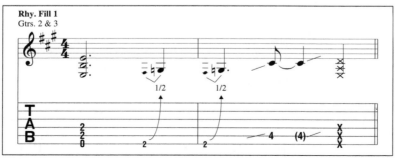

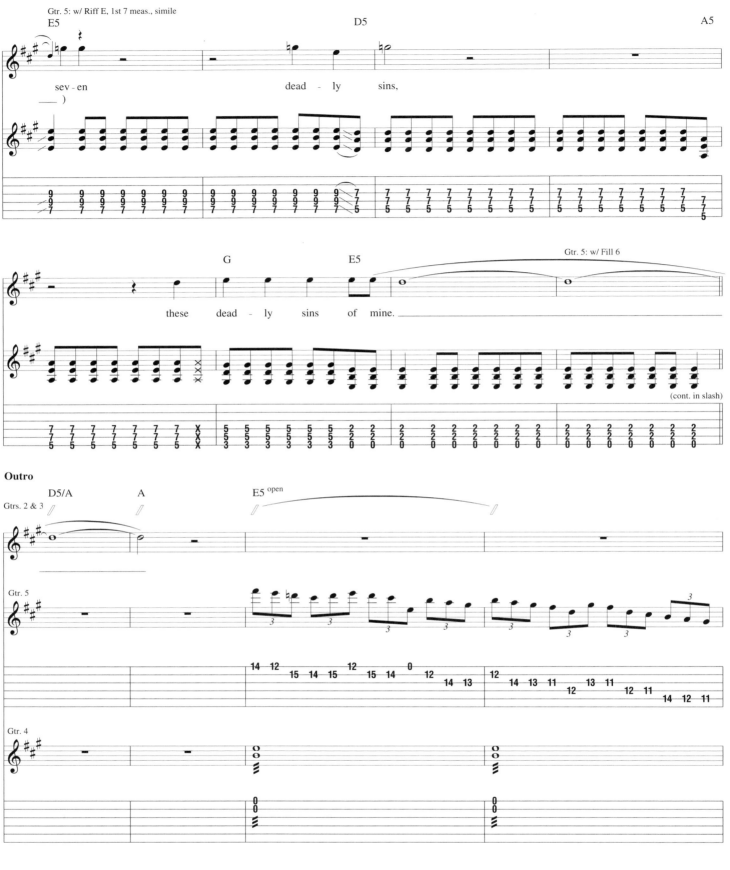

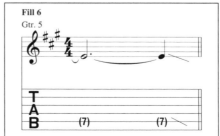

* Randomly scrape the pick up and down the neck
in a fast and furious fashion. (approx. 11 sec.)

Time: The Beginning

Words and Music by Dave Mustaine, Marty Friedman and Bud Prager

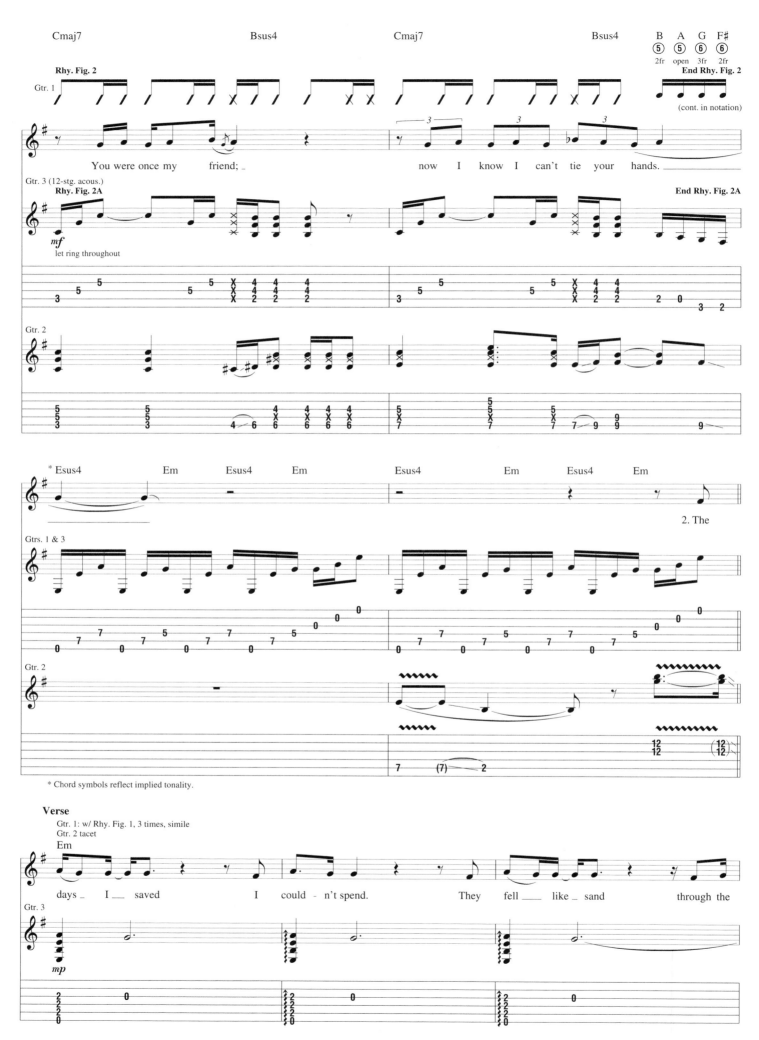

* Chord symbols reflect implied tonality.

Verse

hour - glass.　　　No time ___ to lose,　　　no time to __ choose.

Gtr. 2

mp

* vol. swell

Chorus

** Em　　Em₉⁶　　Em7　　Em　　Cmaj7　　Am9　　B+　　N.C.

Time __ tak - ing time, ___　　　it's ___ tak - en - mine. __

Gtr. 2

p

Gtrs. 1 & 3

Rhy. Fig. 3　　　　　　　　　　　　　　　　　　　　　　End Rhy. Fig. 3

f

** Chord symbols reflect implied tonality.

Gtrs. 1 & 3: w/ Rhy. Fig. 3, 3 times

Em　Em₉⁶　Em7　Em　　Cmaj7　Am9　B+　　N.C.　　Em　Em₉⁶　Em7　Em

___ Scenes _ of __ my life ___　　seem _ so _ un - kind.　　Time　chas - ing time _

Gtr. 2

*** Pluck strings behind nut.

85

creeps up __ be-hind. __ I can't __ run __ for-ev __ er and time waits __ for no

one, __ not e-ven me.

3. An __ en-e-my, I can't de-fend; my

fi - nal place,   a ___ dead - ly end.   Life   is   just   a

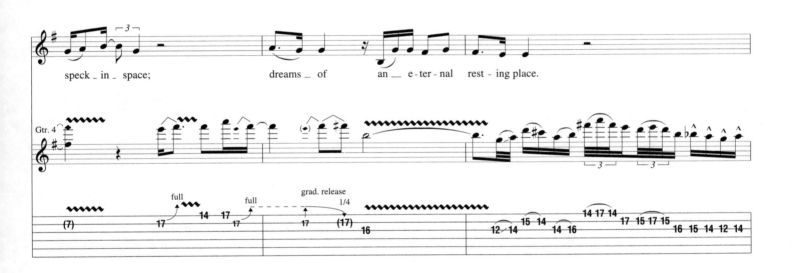

speck _ in _ space;   dreams _ of   an __ e - ter - nal   rest - ing place.

I   can't   get an - y young - er; _____   time   has __ bru - tal hun - ger. _____

* Gtr. 4 to left of slash in TAB.

Chorus

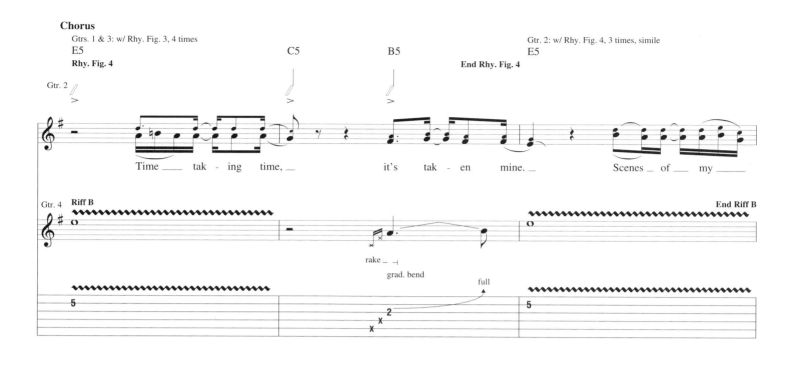

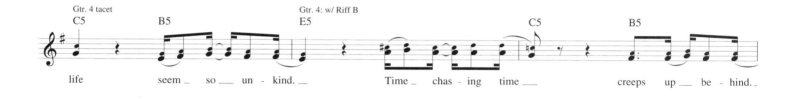

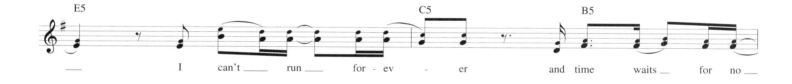

Time: The End

Words and Music by Dave Mustaine and Bud Prager

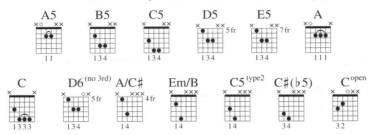

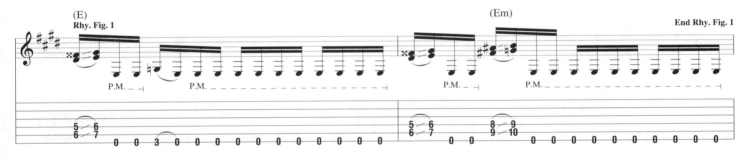

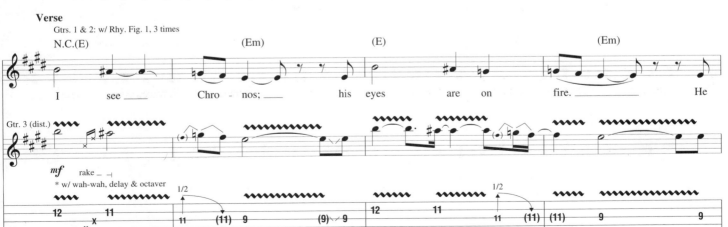

* Octaver set one octave below played pitch.

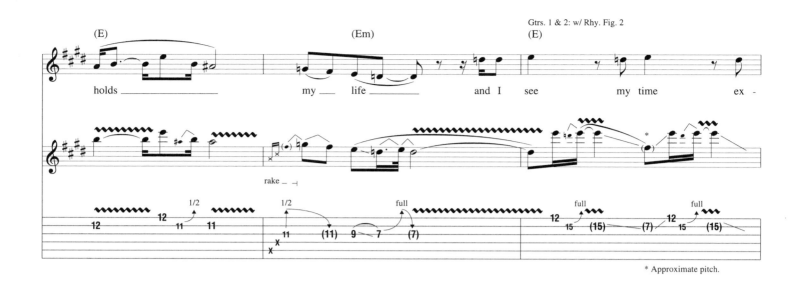

* Approximate pitch.

Chorus

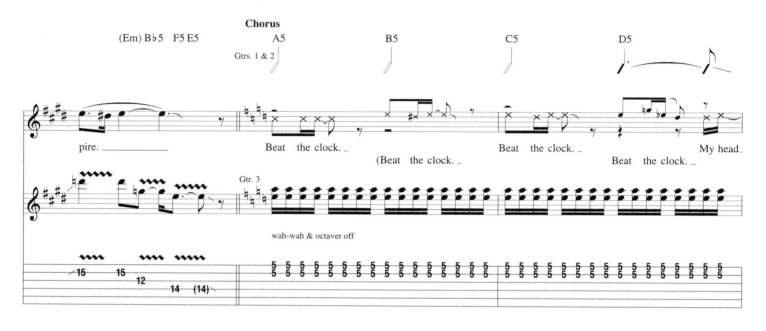

wah-wah & octaver off

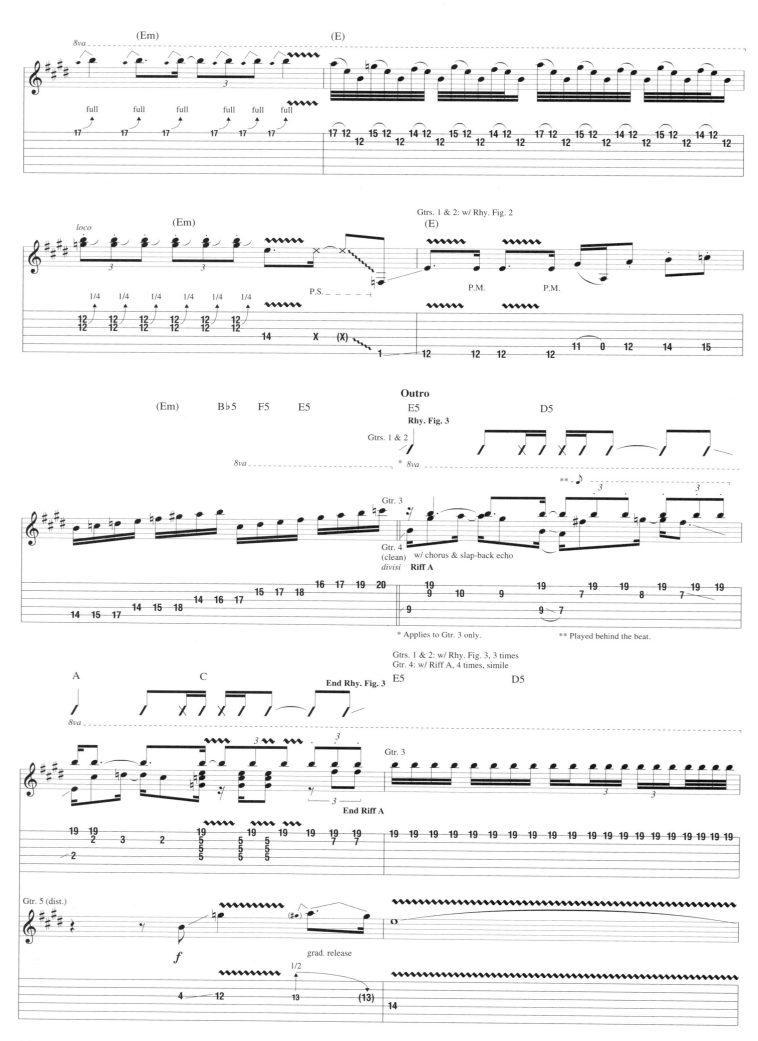

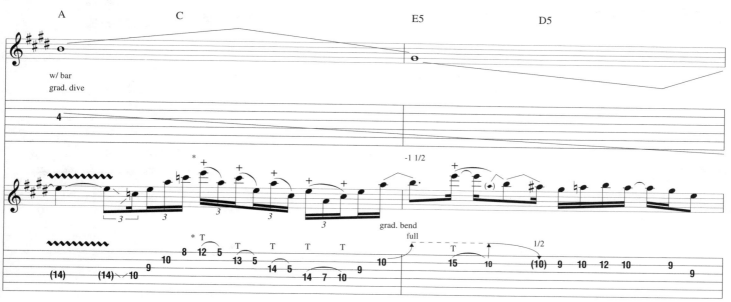

* Tap notes w/ right hand index finger.

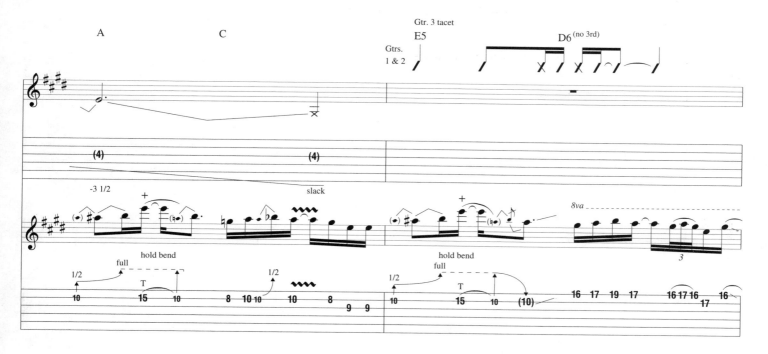

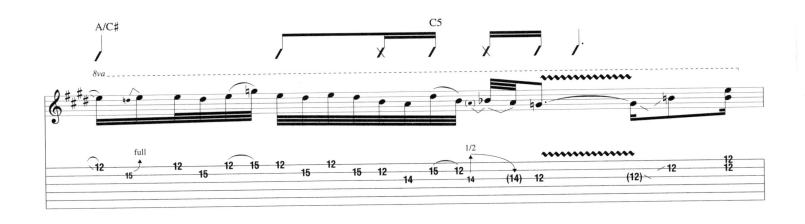

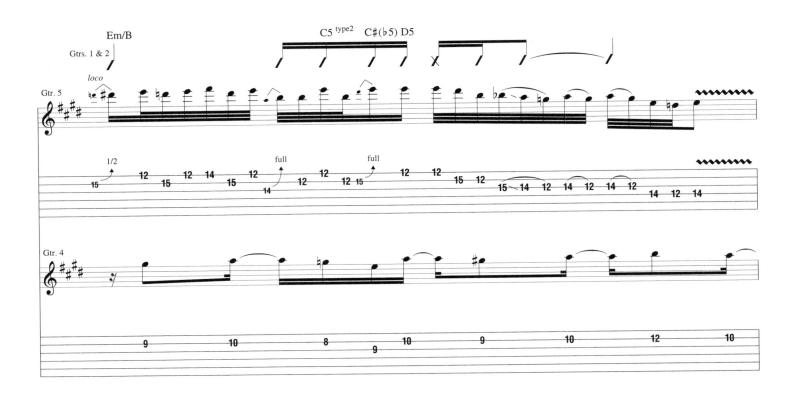

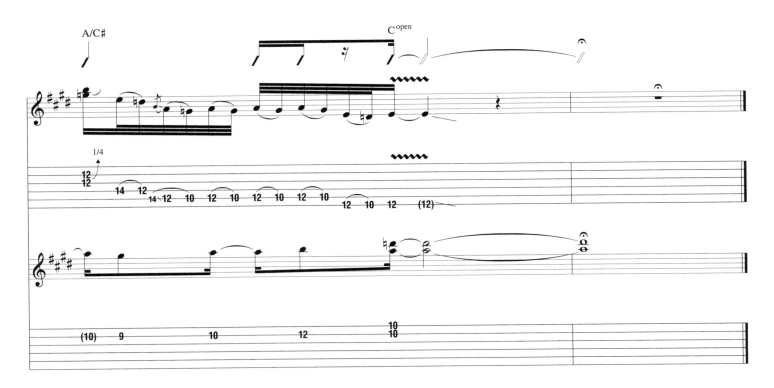

Guitar Notation Legend

Guitar Music can be notated three different ways: on a *musical staff*, in *tablature*, and in *rhythm slashes*.

RHYTHM SLASHES are written above the staff. Strum chords in the rhythm indicated. Use the chord diagrams found at the top of the first page of the transcription for the appropriate chord voicings. Round noteheads indicate single notes.

THE MUSICAL STAFF shows pitches and rhythms and is divided by bar lines into measures. Pitches are named after the first seven letters of the alphabet.

TABLATURE graphically represents the guitar fingerboard. Each horizontal line represents a string, and each number represents a fret.

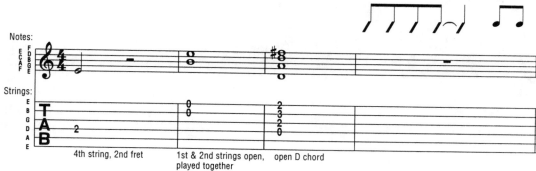

HALF-STEP BEND: Strike the note and bend up 1/2 step.

WHOLE-STEP BEND: Strike the note and bend up one step.

GRACE NOTE BEND: Strike the note and bend up as indicated. The first note does not take up any time.

SLIGHT (MICROTONE) BEND: Strike the note and bend up 1/4 step.

BEND AND RELEASE: Strike the note and bend up as indicated, then release back to the original note. Only the first note is struck.

PRE-BEND: Bend the note as indicated, then strike it.

VIBRATO: The string is vibrated by rapidly bending and releasing the note with the fretting hand.

WIDE VIBRATO: The pitch is varied to a greater degree by vibrating with the fretting hand.

HAMMER-ON: Strike the first (lower) note with one finger, then sound the higher note (on the same string) with another finger by fretting it without picking.

PULL-OFF: Place both fingers on the notes to be sounded. Strike the first note and without picking, pull the finger off to sound the second (lower) note.

LEGATO SLIDE: Strike the first note and then slide the same fret-hand finger up or down to the second note. The second note is not struck.

SHIFT SLIDE: Same as legato slide, except the second note is struck.

TRILL: Very rapidly alternate between the notes indicated by continuously hammering on and pulling off.

TAPPING: Hammer ("tap") the fret indicated with the pick-hand index or middle finger and pull off to the note fretted by the fret hand.

NATURAL HARMONIC: Strike the note while the fret-hand lightly touches the string directly over the fret indicated.

PINCH HARMONIC: The note is fretted normally and a harmonic is produced by adding the edge of the thumb or the tip of the index finger of the pick hand to the normal pick attack.

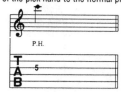

PICK SCRAPE: The edge of the pick is rubbed down (or up) the string, producing a scratchy sound.

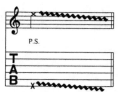

MUFFLED STRINGS: A percussive sound is produced by laying the fret hand across the string(s) without depressing, and striking them with the pick hand.

PALM MUTING: The note is partially muted by the pick hand lightly touching the string(s) just before the bridge.

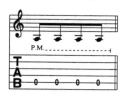

RAKE: Drag the pick across the strings indicated with a single motion.

TREMOLO PICKING: The note is picked as rapidly and continuously as possible.

VIBRATO BAR DIVE AND RETURN: The pitch of the note or chord is dropped a specified number of steps (in rhythm) then returned to the original pitch.

VIBRATO BAR SCOOP: Depress the bar just before striking the note, then quickly release the bar.

VIBRATO BAR DIP: Strike the note and then immediately drop a specified number of steps, then release back to the original pitch.

RECORDED VERSIONS
The Best Note-For-Note Transcriptions Available

ALL BOOKS INCLUDE TABLATURE

00690016 Will Ackerman Collection $19.95	00694807 Danny Gatton – 88 Elmira St $19.95	00690055 Red Hot Chili Peppers –
00690199 Aerosmith – Nine Lives $19.95	00690127 Goo Goo Dolls – A Boy Named Goo $19.95	Bloodsugarsexmagik $19.95
00690146 Aerosmith – Toys in the Attic $19.95	00690338 Goo Goo Dolls – Dizzy Up the Girl $19.95	00690379 Red Hot Chili Peppers – Californication ..$19.95
00694865 Alice In Chains – Dirt $19.95	00690117 John Gorka Collection $19.95	00690090 Red Hot Chili Peppers – One Hot Minute ..$22.95
00694932 Allman Brothers Band – Volume 1 ....$24.95	00690114 Buddy Guy Collection Vol. A-J $22.95	00694892 Guitar Style Of Jerry Reed $19.95
00694933 Allman Brothers Band – Volume 2 ....$24.95	00690193 Buddy Guy Collection Vol. L-Y $22.95	00694937 Jimmy Reed – Master Bluesman $19.95
00694934 Allman Brothers Band – Volume 3 ....$24.95	00694798 George Harrison Anthology $19.95	00694899 R.E.M. – Automatic For The People ...$19.95
00694877 Chet Atkins – Guitars For All Seasons $19.95	00690068 Return Of The Hellecasters $19.95	00690260 Jimmie Rodgers Guitar Collection $17.95
00694918 Randy Bachman Collection $22.95	00692930 Jimi Hendrix – Are You Experienced? ..$24.95	00690014 Rolling Stones – Exile On Main Street ..$24.95
00694880 Beatles – Abbey Road $19.95	00692931 Jimi Hendrix – Axis: Bold As Love $22.95	00690186 Rolling Stones – Rock & Roll Circus ...$19.95
00694863 Beatles –	00692932 Jimi Hendrix – Electric Ladyland $24.95	00690135 Otis Rush Collection $19.95
Sgt. Pepper's Lonely Hearts Club Band ..$19.95	00690218 Jimi Hendrix – First Rays of the New Rising Sun $24.95	00690031 Santana's Greatest Hits $19.95
00690383 Beatles – Yellow Submarine $19.95	00690038 Gary Hoey – Best Of $19.95	00694805 Scorpions – Crazy World $19.95
00690174 Beck – Mellow Gold $17.95	00660029 Buddy Holly $19.95	00690150 Son Seals – Bad Axe Blues $17.95
00690346 Beck – Mutations $19.95	00660169 John Lee Hooker – A Blues Legend $19.95	00690128 Seven Mary Three – American Standards ..$19.95
00690175 Beck – Odelay $17.95	00690054 Hootie & The Blowfish –	00690076 Sex Pistols – Never Mind The Bollocks ..$19.95
00694884 The Best of George Benson $19.95	Cracked Rear View $19.95	00120105 Kenny Wayne Shepherd – Ledbetter Heights $19.95
00692385 Chuck Berry $19.95	00694905 Howlin' Wolf $19.95	00120123 Kenny Wayne Shepherd – Trouble Is ...$19.95
00692200 Black Sabbath –	00690136 Indigo Girls – 1200 Curfews $22.95	00690196 Silverchair – Freak Show $19.95
We Sold Our Soul For Rock 'N' Roll $19.95	00694938 Elmore James –	00690130 Silverchair – Frogstomp $19.95
00690115 Blind Melon – Soup $19.95	Master Electric Slide Guitar $19.95	00690041 Smithereens – Best Of $19.95
00690305 Blink 182 – Dude Ranch $19.95	00690167 Skip James Blues Guitar Collection ...$16.95	00694885 Spin Doctors – Pocket Full Of Kryptonite ..$19.95
00690028 Blue Oyster Cult – Cult Classics $19.95	00694833 Billy Joel For Guitar $19.95	00690124 Sponge – Rotting Pinata $19.95
00690219 Blur $19.95	00694912 Eric Johnson – Ah Via Musicom $19.95	00694921 Steppenwolf, The Best Of $22.95
00694935 Boston: Double Shot Of $22.95	00690169 Eric Johnson – Venus Isle $22.95	00694957 Rod Stewart – Acoustic Live $22.95
00690237 Meredith Brooks – Blurring the Edges ..$19.95	00694799 Robert Johnson – At The Crossroads ..$19.95	00690021 Sting – Fields Of Gold $19.95
00690168 Roy Buchanon Collection $19.95	00693185 Judas Priest – Vintage Hits $19.95	00690242 Suede – Coming Up $19.95
00690364 Cake – Songbook $19.95	00690277 Best of Kansas $19.95	00694824 Best Of James Taylor $16.95
00690337 Jerry Cantrell – Boggy Depot $19.95	00690073 B. B. King – 1950-1957 ....$24.95	00690238 Third Eye Blind $19.95
00690293 Best of Steven Curtis Chapman $19.95	00690098 B. B. King – 1958-1967 ....$24.95	00690267 311 ....$19.95
00690043 Cheap Trick – Best Of $19.95	00690134 Freddie King Collection $17.95	00690030 Toad The Wet Sprocket $19.95
00690171 Chicago – Definitive Guitar Collection ..$22.95	00694903 The Best Of Kiss $24.95	00690228 Tonic – Lemon Parade $19.95
00690393 Eric Clapton – Selections from Blues ..$19.95	00690157 Kiss – Alive $19.95	00690295 Tool – Aenima $19.95
00660139 Eric Clapton – Journeyman $19.95	00690163 Mark Knopfler/Chet Atkins – Neck and Neck $19.95	00699191 The Best of U2 – 1980-1990 ....$19.95
00694869 Eric Clapton – Live Acoustic $19.95	00690296 Patty Larkin Songbook $17.95	00694411 U2 – The Joshua Tree $19.95
00694896 John Mayall/Eric Clapton – Bluesbreakers $19.95	00690070 Live – Throwing Copper $19.95	00690039 Steve Vai – Alien Love Secrets $24.95
00690162 Best of the Clash $19.95	00690018 Living Colour – Best Of $19.95	00690172 Steve Vai – Fire Garden $24.95
00690166 Albert Collins – The Alligator Years ..$16.95	00694845 Yngwie Malmsteen – Fire And Ice ...$19.95	00690023 Jimmie Vaughan – Strange Pleasures ..$19.95
00694940 Counting Crows – August & Everything After $19.95	00694956 Bob Marley – Legend $19.95	00690370 Stevie Ray Vaughan and Double Trouble –
00690197 Counting Crows – Recovering the Satellites ..$19.95	00690283 Best of Sarah McLachlan $19.95	The Real Deal: Greatest Hits Volume 2 ...$22.95
00690118 Cranberries – The Best of $19.95	00690382 Sarah McLachlan – Mirrorball $19.95	00660136 Stevie Ray Vaughan – In Step $19.95
00690215 Music of Robert Cray $19.95	00690354 Sarah McLachlan – Surfacing $19.95	00694835 Stevie Ray Vaughan – The Sky Is Crying ..$19.95
00694840 Cream – Disraeli Gears $19.95	00690239 Matchbox 20 – Yourself or Someone Like You ..$19.95	00694776 Vaughan Brothers – Family Style $19.95
00690352 Creed – My Own Pirson $19.95	00690244 Megadeath – Cryptic Writings $19.95	00690217 Verve Pipe, The – Villains $19.95
00690007 Danzig 4 ....$19.95	00690236 Mighty Mighty Bosstones – Let's Face It ..$19.95	00120026 Joe Walsh – Look What I Did... ......$24.95
00690184 dc Talk – Jesus Freak $19.95	00690040 Steve Miller Band Greatest Hits $19.95	00694789 Muddy Waters – Deep Blues $24.95
00690333 dc Talk – Supernatural $19.95	00694802 Gary Moore – Still Got The Blues $19.95	00690071 Weezer $19.95
00660186 Alex De Grassi Guitar Collection $19.95	00694958 Mountain, Best Of $19.95	00690286 Weezer – Pinkerton $19.95
00690289 Best of Deep Purple $17.95	00694913 Nirvana – In Utero $19.95	00694970 Who, The – Definitive Collection A-E ..$24.95
00694831 Derek And The Dominos –	00694883 Nirvana – Nevermind $19.95	00694971 Who, The – Definitive Collection F-Li ..$24.95
Layla & Other Assorted Love Songs ...$19.95	00690026 Nirvana – Acoustic In New York $19.95	00694972 Who, The – Definitive Collection Lo-R ..$24.95
00690322 Ani Di Franco – Little Plastic Castle $19.95	00690121 Oasis – (What's The Story) Morning Glory $19.95	00694973 Who, The – Definitive Collection S-Y ...$24.95
00690187 Dire Straits – Brothers In Arms $19.95	00690290 Offspring, The – Ignition $19.95	00690320 Best of Dar Williams $17.95
00690191 Dire Straits – Money For Nothing $24.95	00690204 Offspring, The – Ixnay on the Hombre ..$17.95	00690319 Best of Stevie Wonder $19.95
00695382 The Very Best of Dire Straits –	00690203 Offspring, The – Smash $17.95	00690319 Stevie Wonder – Some of the Best ...$19.95
Sultans of Swing $19.95	00694830 Ozzy Osbourne – No More Tears $19.95	
00660178 Willie Dixon – Master Blues Composer ..$24.95	00694855 Pearl Jam – Ten $19.95	
00690250 Best of Duane Eddy $16.95	00690053 Liz Phair – Whip Smart $19.95	
00690349 Eve 6 ....$19.95	00690176 Phish – Billy Breathes $22.95	
00690323 Fastball – All the Pain Money Can Buy ..$19.95	00690331 Phish – The Story of Ghost $19.95	
00690089 Foo Fighters $19.95	00693800 Pink Floyd – Early Classics $19.95	
00690235 Foo Fighters – The Colour and the Shape ..$19.95	00694967 Police – Message In A Box Boxed Set ...$70.00	
00690394 Foo Fighters –	00694974 Queen – A Night At The Opera $19.95	
There Is Nothing Left to Lose $19.95	00690395 Rage Against The Machine –	
00694920 Free – Best Of $18.95	The Battle of Los Angeles $19.95	
00690324 Fuel – Sunburn $19.95	00690145 Rage Against The Machine – Evil Empire ..$19.95	
00690222 G3 Live – Satriani, Vai, Johnson $22.95	00690179 Rancid – And Out Come the Wolves ...$22.95	